WOOF
AND THE
NEW NEIGHBORS

by Danae Dobson
Illustrated by Dee deRosa

WORD PUBLISHING
Dallas · London · Sydney · Singapore

For my "little" brother, Ryan,
who is now bigger than his sister.
He was there in the car pool
when our Dad created the character of Woof,
and we both fell for that ugly, old mutt at the same time.
Now Ryan is a college student, and I'm proud to be his sister.

Woof and the New Neighbors

Copyright ©1989 by Danae Dobson for the text. Copyright ©1989 by Dee deRosa for the illustrations.
All rights reserved. No portion of this book may be reproduced in any form without the written permission
of the publishers, except for brief quotations in reviews.
Scripture quotation is from *The Living Bible, Paraphrased,* copyright 1971 by Tyndale House Publishers,
Wheaton, IL. Used by permission.
Library of Congress Cataloging-in-Publication Data
Dobson, Danae.
  Woof and the new neighbors.
  Summary: Mark, Krissy, and their dog Woof learn to be kind to their enemies, even when they are their
mischievous, next-door neighbors.
  [1. Neighborliness — Fiction. 2. Behavior — Fiction. 3. Dogs — Fiction. 4. Christian life — Fiction.]
I. DeRosa, Dee, ill. II. Title.
PZ7.D6614Wr 1989   [E]   89-22559
ISBN 0-8499-8349-5

Printed in the United States of America
9801239KRU987654321

A MESSAGE FROM
Dr. James Dobson

Before you read about this dog named Woof perhaps you would like to know how these books came to be written. When my children, Danae and Ryan, were young, I often told them stories at bedtime. Many of those tales were about pet animals who were loved by people like those in our own family. Later, I created more stories while driving the children to school in our car pool. The kids began to fall in love with these pets, even though they existed only in our minds. I found out just how much they loved these animals when I made the mistake of telling them a story in which one of their favorite pets died. There were so many tears I had to bring him back to life!

These tales made a special impression on Danae. At the age of twelve, she decided to write her own book about her favorite animal, Woof, and see if Word Publishers would like to print it. She did, and they did, and in the process she became the youngest author in Word's history. Now, ten years later, Danae has written five more, totally new adventures with Woof and the Petersons. And she is still Word's youngest author!

Danae has discovered a talent God has given her, and it all started with our family spending time together, talking about a dog and the two children who loved him. We hope that not only will you enjoy Woof's adventures but that you and your family will enjoy the time spent reading them together. Perhaps you also will discover a talent God has given you.

It was a warm Saturday morning as the Peterson family sat down to breakfast.

"Guess what?" said six-year-old Mark, reaching for the orange juice. "Barney said some people bought the house next door and they're moving in today."

Father smiled as he turned a page of the newspaper. "That's good," he said warmly. "That house has been empty for six months. It will be nice to have some new neighbors."

Just then, the conversation was interrupted by a shaggy-haired mutt with a crooked hind leg and one floppy ear. He came bounding into the room with a red ball in his mouth and placed it down by the children's feet, as if wanting to play.

"Not now, Woof," ten-year-old Krissy laughed.

"Maybe later, boy," said Mark, patting his furry friend on the head. Woof stayed near the table, hoping a bite of food would drop off.

"I hope the new family next door will have kids our age," said Krissy.

"I can't wait to see what they're like," said Mark.

"It would be nice if you would be there to greet them when they arrive," suggested Mother. "I'm sure they would like that."

The two children agreed and went outside to play catch with Woof.

An hour later a huge, yellow moving van pulled up in front of the house next door. Mark and Krissy stopped their game and watched as the tires screeched to a stop at the curb. The van was followed by an old pick-up truck that carried three passengers. They turned into the driveway.

"Boy! That truck looks familiar," said Krissy, straining her eyes to get a closer look.

The moving van then backed into the driveway and hid the truck from view.

"Come on!" said Mark, grabbing his sister by the sleeve. "Let's get a closer look."

The two children moved nearer to the van and stood by an oak tree in their yard. Even Woof seemed curious as he followed at their heels, looking anxiously at the large vehicle.

The children could hear voices and doors being opened and shut. Soon a husky man walked in front of the van, carrying two boxes to the front door. Again, Mark and Krissy thought something looked familiar.

"Now wait a minute," Mark whispered. "Haven't we seen that man before?"

Krissy shrugged her shoulders and frowned. "I think so. There's something strange about all this."

Suddenly Woof growled and began to bark loudly.

"What is it, boy?" Mark asked.

The hair on the dog's back stood straight up, and his eyes were fixed in front of him. In a few seconds two young boys walked past the van and up the driveway. Mark and Krissy looked at one another and gasped out loud. "THE HARPER TWINS!" they shouted at the same time.

Woof continued to bark. He remembered those boys very well. They had hit him in the shoulder with a rock at a service station last summer. He had been sore for four days, and he was still angry about it.

"I can't believe it!" Mark exclaimed. "Those awful Harper twins are moving in *next door!*"

"Come on. Let's go tell Mom and Dad," Krissy said.

The two children ran through the front door and into the living room, with Woof close behind.

"What's the matter?" Father asked, putting on his glasses.

Mark caught his breath and said, "Do you remember when we were traveling to visit Grandma and two mean boys threw a rock at Woof while we were at the gas station?"

Mr. and Mrs. Peterson nodded.

Those boys are our *new neighbors*!" Krissy wailed.

The two parents frowned in disbelief.

"Are you sure?" Mother asked.

"Yes!" Mark and Krissy said at the same time.

"Come look out the window and you'll see!" said Krissy.

Woof continued to growl as the Peterson family drew back the curtain and peered through the glass. In the distance they could see two scruffy-looking boys in matching overalls unloading more boxes from the van.

"They *are* the Harper twins!" Father said.

"What should we do?" Mark asked.

"You should do what any neighborly person *would* do," Mother suggested. "Go over and say hello." Mrs. Peterson noticed the unhappy look on their faces. "Go on," she repeated. "Wouldn't you want to be welcomed if you moved into a new neighborhood?"

The two children looked at one another. "I suppose we should," Krissy said. "Come on, Mark, let's go."

The two children and Woof went back into the yard and over to the big, yellow van. Woof was still stiff-legged and tense. In a few moments the twins came out of the house to get another load. They stopped quickly when they saw Mark and Krissy, and they had a very surprised look on their faces.

Krissy cleared her throat. "Hello," she said in a friendly tone of voice. "I suppose you remember us from the gas station awhile back."

The boys did not answer but continued with their work.

"I'm Mark Peterson, and this is Krissy," said Mark. "And I'm sure you remember Woof," he chuckled.

The two boys still did not answer. Finally, one of them said, "This here's Billy, and I'm Bobby. And over there in the corner is old Butch."

The Peterson children looked over at the large bulldog that was tied to the gate.

"You best keep your mutt away from old Butch," Bobby sneered. "He just might make a meal out of him." With that, the two boys burst out laughing.

Woof growled angrily at the twins. He never would have tried to hurt them, but he knew these boys were troublemakers.

The twins continued to laugh as Mark and Krissy turned and went back to the house. They were very upset at how the boys had treated them, but they were even *more* upset that Billy and Bobby Harper were there to stay!

That night as the Peterson children were getting ready for bed, Father came upstairs to say good-night.

"Why did those Harper twins have to move in next door?" Krissy complained.

"They may be nicer than you think," said Father. "But if I were you, I'd stay away from them for a while. Maybe you can make friends with them later. And keep Woof away from their dog, Mark! He looks pretty mean."

After the children had said their prayers, Mother tucked them in bed
with a kiss on each cheek. In a few minutes both Mark and Krissy were
fast asleep. But it wasn't long before the entire Peterson family was
awakened by a strange sound outside. It was not a crash or a whistle.
What they heard was a clanking noise.

Woof was down the stairs in seconds, clawing at the front door to get
out. He wanted to protect his territory.

"What was that?" Krissy asked nervously.

"I don't know," Mark replied.

Again and again, the sound came from the front yard, and it seemed to
be moving. Mr. and Mrs. Peterson met the children at the foot of the stairs.

"Everyone stay inside," Father instructed. "I'm going with Woof to see
who or what is out there."

"Be careful," Mrs. Peterson warned.

In a couple of minutes, Father returned to the house.

"What is it?" Mark and Krissy asked impatiently.

"Someone tied a string of tin cans to a cat's tail," he said with disgust. "The poor animal is scared to death. I came back to get some scissors to cut the string."

Mark and Krissy went outside with him as he cut the string of cans off the frightened cat. The poor kitty climbed up the nearest tree after he was released.

"I bet I know who did this," said Krissy angrily. "It was Billy and Bobby Harper!"

"Maybe it was," agreed her father, "but you don't know they were responsible for it. Let's all just go back to bed now and get some rest."

The Peterson family was soon fast asleep again, but Woof was still tense. He lay awake the entire night at the foot of Mark's bed, waiting for more trouble to occur. But the rest of the night was peaceful.

When morning came, the Petersons put on their nicest clothes to go to church. "Come on, everyone. We don't want to be late," Father called from the bottom of the staircase.

The children gathered up their belongings and Bibles and headed for the car.

"Good-bye, Woof," Mark said, patting his dog on the head. "Sorry you can't come with us."

Woof watched as the family climbed into the car and drove down the street. He was still on the porch when something caught his eye! Billy and Bobby Harper were creeping along the side of their house. Each of them was holding a small object in his hand. Woof didn't know they were slingshots, but he knew the boys were up to no good. Woof followed the twins at close range as they ran and hid behind a bush in a neighbor's yard.

In a few seconds one of the boys stood up and placed a rock in his slingshot. He then pulled it back and aimed. In a flash the rock flew through the air and crashed through a window of Mrs. Perry's house. The impact sent glass shattering in all directions, and you could hear Mrs. Perry's scream all the way down the street. By the time she got to the front yard, the boys had made their escape.

Some neighbors heard the noise and came out to their front yards, but no one had seen who broke the window. No one, that is, except Woof! But there was nothing he could do. He couldn't tell anyone who was guilty, even though he understood the boys had done wrong. All he could do was trot back home.

When the Peterson family returned, they heard about Mrs. Perry's broken window. Mark and Krissy suspected the Harper twins, but their father pointed out it could have been an accident.

Woof was becoming more and more upset. He was angry about all the trouble the boys were causing around the neighborhood, but he just didn't know what to do. As he walked around the backyard, he decided to get a drink from his water dish. But no sooner had he begun lapping the liquid than he spit it out again — hacking and coughing.

As Mark walked outside, he saw Woof coughing and picked up the dish to see what was wrong. "This smells like vinegar!" he exclaimed. "Those nasty twins must have ruined the water with vinegar!"

When Mark told his parents what the boys had done, they were also upset. "This certainly wasn't an accident," Mr. Peterson said. "I think it's time I had a talk with the boys' father. I'm going over there right now."

Mr. Peterson walked up the porch steps and rang the doorbell. The husky man came to the door. "What can I do fer you?" he asked.

After introducing himself and shaking hands, Mr. Peterson explained about the problems that had been occurring in the neighborhood.

But before he could finish the story, Mr. Harper interrupted him, angrily. "Are you sayin' you think my boys is responsible fer all this?" he asked.

"Well...I..." Mr. Peterson was taken by surprise.

"My boys is good kids. Ain't no way they'd be doin' them awful things. Mister, I reckon you got the wrong house." With that, he shut the door.

As Mr. Peterson was walking away, he could see Billy and Bobby Harper snickering by the window. "Those naughty boys . . ." he murmured to himself.

Mark was putting some fresh water in Woof's dish when his father returned.

"What happened, Dad?" he asked.

Mr. Peterson just shook his head. "Mr. Harper didn't help," Father said. "We will just have to be more watchful."

For the next two days, there were constant complaints around the neighborhood. Mark's friend Barney Martin found a flat tire on his bicycle when he was ready to leave for school. Then Mrs. McCurry noticed her daisies had been trampled. Mr. Gosset discovered his big tree had been covered with wet toilet paper, and a "For Sale" sign had been moved from a nearby house. The neighbors around Maple Street were in an uproar! But who was to blame? No one had seen the culprits.

One afternoon while the Peterson family was away with some friends, Woof stretched out behind their house in the sun. He was waiting for the children to return so he could go for a walk or play a game of catch. The warmth of the sun felt good on his back.

Suddenly Woof's ears perked up! A hissing noise had come from the Petersons' garage! Woof trotted over to the side door to investigate. Slowly he peered around the corner to see what had caused the funny noise. There, crouched low by the Petersons' car, were Billy and Bobby Harper. They had let the air out of three tires! The two boys didn't see Woof as they crept over to the last tire to finish the job.

Woof knew he had to think fast. This would be a perfect opportunity to catch the boys, but how was he going to keep them in the garage until the Petersons returned? Nervously, Woof looked around the doorway. There, above him, was his chance! A tiny latch hung just within his reach.

Quickly Woof nudged the door shut and pushed the latch with his paw. The Harper twins were trapped inside!

"Let us out of here!" the boys yelled, banging on the door with their fists. Woof stood guard by the door, pacing back and forth and barking to summon help. But the Petersons had not returned home yet.

Suddenly Woof sensed he was in great danger. He wheeled around to see Butch charging toward him. The dog had heard the boys' cries for help, and he was rushing to their rescue. He bolted toward Woof with all his might.

Woof backed up against the door of the garage and braced himself for the attack. But just before the angry bulldog reached him, a voice called from across the yard.

"Butch! Come here!" Mr. Harper commanded.

The bulldog stopped in his tracks when he heard his name called.

"I said to come here *now*," Mr. Harper repeated. Old Butch had obviously given up the fight as he turned and headed back toward his master. "I *thought* I saw you leave the yard a minute ago. What are you doing here?" Mr. Harper asked, grabbing his pet by the collar.

Woof was greatly relieved that Butch had been called off. That could have been a terrible fight.

Just then, the Peterson family returned in their friends' car.

"What's going on out here?" Mr. Peterson asked, as he walked up the driveway.

Before he could get an answer, a loud noise came from the garage.

"What was *that*?" asked Krissy.

"It sounds like someone banging on the garage door," said Mother.

As the Petersons and Mr. Harper hurried toward the garage, they could hear voices inside.

"Let us out of here!" the boys yelled, continuing to bang on the door.

Woof stood guard as Mr. Peterson unlatched the lock that held them captive. As soon as they were free, Billy and Bobby Harper pushed their way out the door and into the yard. Their faces were hot and sweaty from being locked in the stuffy garage, and their hands were black from tampering with the tires.

"What's going on? What are you two boys doing in here?" Mr. Peterson asked sternly.

The twins did not answer, but they had a very guilty look on their faces. Just then, Krissy gasped as she peered through the door of the garage.

"Why, they let the air out of our tires!" she exclaimed.

The boys cast their eyes toward the ground as everyone looked to see the damage that had been done.

"Did you boys do this?" asked Mr. Harper.

"Yes, Pa, we done it," answered Bobby, who still hadn't looked up as he studied the ground.

"Don't you think you owe these people an apology?" his father asked.

"We're sorry," said the twins at the same time.

"Now get on home, you two!" ordered Mr. Harper.

With that, the boys took off running back toward their house.

"I'm awful sorry about what my sons done to yer car," said Mr. Harper apologetically. "I'm also sorry for not believin' you when you was sayin' my boys was causin' trouble. But I'll deal with them about this."

"I'd appreciate that," said Mr. Peterson, extending his hand toward his neighbor. "And I hope we can be friends."

Mr. Harper smiled, and the men shook hands.

"Well, come on, Butch. Let's go," he said, motioning toward the gate.

The Petersons watched as Mr. Harper and his dog disappeared around the corner.

"I think Woof was the one who trapped the Harper twins in the garage!" exclaimed Mark, patting his dog on the head.

"Woof sure is a *good* dog," said Krissy.

"But I don't understand why you let Billy and Bobby Harper off so easily," said Mark, looking up toward his father. "You didn't even get mad at them."

Father explained his reasoning. "Well, first of all, it is their father's place to discipline them. But there's another lesson to be learned from this experience. We'll talk about it after dinner tonight."

That evening before bedtime Mr. Peterson and the children read these words spoken by Jesus nearly 2000 years ago: "'There is a saying, "Love your friends and hate your enemies." But I say, Love your enemies! Pray for those who persecute you! In that way you will be acting as true sons of your Father in heaven.' That means Jesus wants us to love everyone," said Mr. Peterson.

"He even wants His children to be friendly with people who are not very nice. Believe it or not, God loves the Harper twins as much as He does us, even though He doesn't like some of the things they do."

"How could God love *those* boys?" asked Mark.

"Well, look at it this way," said Father. "Have you ever seen a mother at the Harper home?"

"No," said Krissy. "What do you think happened to her?"

"I don't know," said Father. "But they are having to grow up without a mother to love and care for them. There is a *reason* for their mischief, and we can only guess why they are like they are. I believe they've had a pretty rough childhood. Whatever the cause, God knows about it and wants us to try to tell them about Jesus. Maybe we'll get that chance someday."

"I understand!" said Mark. "We'll never be able to tell them about Jesus if we stay mad at them all the time."

"That's right," said Mr. Peterson.

Mark and Krissy had a better attitude about their new neighbors after talking with their father.

Woof didn't understand all those words, but he sure liked being in the Peterson family.

From
Grandpa Oliver
Grandma Emma 8/94